W9-CLD-356

Story Time with Signs & Rhymes

Wear a Silly Hat
Sign Language for Clothing

by Dawn Babb Prochovnic
illustrated by Stephanie Bauer

Content Consultant:
William Vicars, EdD, Director of Lifeprint Institute
and Associate Professor, ASL & Deaf Studies
California State University, Sacramento

magic Wagon

For Nikko, who dresses my heart with silliness and sunshine—DP
For Riley and Lottie . . . my dress-up queens—SB

Published by Magic Wagon, a division of the ABDO Group, 8000 West 78th Street, Edina, Minnesota 55439.

Printed in the United States.

 PRINTED ON RECYCLED PAPER

Written by Dawn Babb Prochovnic
Illustrations by Stephanie Bauer
Edited by Stephanie Hedlund and Rochelle Baltzer
Cover and Interior layout and design by Neil Klinepier

Story Time with Signs & Rhymes provides an introduction to ASL vocabulary through stories that are written and structured in English. ASL is a separate language with its own structure. Just as there are personal and regional variations in spoken and written languages, there are similar variations in sign language.

Library of Congress Cataloging-in-Publication Data

Prochovnic, Dawn Babb.
  Wear a silly hat : sign language for clothing / by Dawn Babb Prochovnic ; illustrated by Stephanie Bauer ; content consultant, William Vicars.
    p. cm. -- (Story time with signs & rhymes)
  Includes "alphabet handshapes;" American Sign Language glossary, fun facts, and activities; further reading and web sites.
  ISBN 978-1-60270-674-3
  [1. Stories in rhyme. 2. Clothing and dress--Fiction. 3. English language--Adjective. 4. American Sign Language. 5. Vocabulary.] I. Bauer, Stephanie, ill. II. Title.
  PZ8.3.P93654We 2009
  [E]--dc22
                                                                            2009002403

Alphabet Handshapes

American Sign Language (ASL) is a visual language that uses handshapes, movements, and facial expressions. Sometimes people spell English words by making the handshape for each letter in the word they want to sign. This is called fingerspelling. The pictures below show the handshapes for each letter in the manual alphabet.

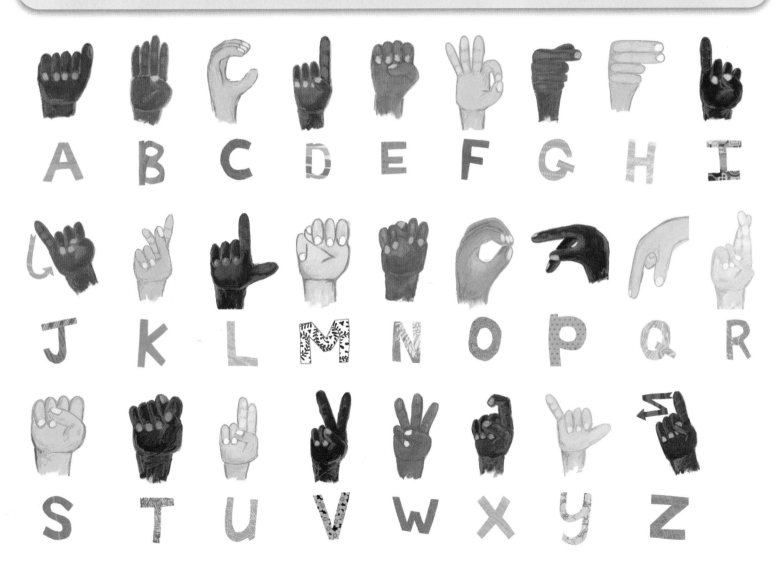

If your **pants** are purple, wear a silly hat.
If you're purple in the **pants**, wear a hat that makes you dance.
If your **pants** are purple, wear a silly hat.

pants

5

If your **dress** is frilly, wear a royal hat.

If you're frilly in the **dress**, then your hat should wow your guests.

If your **dress** is frilly, wear a royal hat.

dress

If your **coat** is soggy, wear a mighty hat.
If you're soggy in the **coat**, then your hat can sail a boat.
If your **coat** is soggy, wear a mighty hat.

coat

If your **boots** are muddy, wear a flowered hat.
If you're muddy in the **boots**, then your hat should have some roots.
If your **boots** are muddy, wear a flowered hat.

boots

If your **gloves** are sparkly, wear a magic hat.
If you're sparkly in the **gloves**, wear a hat that hatches doves.
If your **gloves** are sparkly, wear a magic hat.

gloves

If your **shorts** are stripey, wear a jungle hat.
If you're stripey in the **shorts**, wear a hat that roars and snorts.
If your **shorts** are stripey, wear a jungle hat.

14

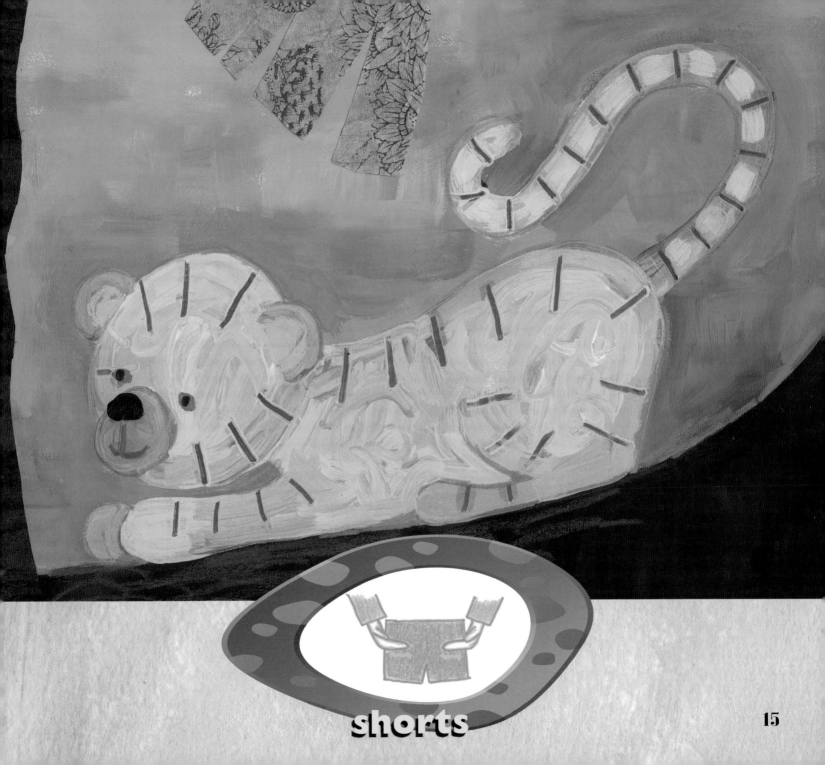

shorts

If your **vest** is spiffy, wear a shiny hat.
If you're spiffy in the **vest**, then your hat should look its best.
If your **vest** is spiffy, wear a shiny hat.

16

vest

If your **socks** are springy, wear a groovy hat.

If you're springy in the **socks**, you should wear a hat that rocks.

If your **socks** are springy, wear a groovy hat.

18

socks

19

If your **shirt** is messy, wear a yummy hat.
If you're messy in the **shirt**, then your hat can make dessert.
If your **shirt** is messy, wear a yummy hat.

shirt

If your **pack** is heavy, wear a sturdy hat.
If you're heavy in the **pack**, then your hat can ease your back.
If your **pack** is heavy, wear a sturdy hat.

pack

If your **shoes** are fancy, wear your favorite hat.
If you're wearing fancy **shoes**, wear whatever hat you choose.
If your **shoes** are fancy, wear your favorite hat.

24

shoes

If your **robe** is sleepy, wear a dreamy hat.
If your **robe** is sleepy tight, wear a hat that says, "goodnight."
If your **robe** is sleepy, wear a dreamy hat.

26

robe

American Sign Language Glossary

 **boots:** First do the sign for "shoes." Now hold your left arm in front of your body with your palm facing down, and tap your right hand on the middle of your left arm. It should look like you are showing that your "shoes" go up to your knees.

 **coat:** Touch the thumbs of both "A Hands" to your shoulders. Now, slide your thumbs down toward the middle of your body. It should look like you are pulling your coat over your shoulders.

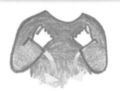 **dress:** Touch the thumbs of your "Five Hands" to the top of your chest. Now, brush your thumbs down your chest and away from your body. It should look like you are showing the shape and length of a dress.

 **gloves:** Hold your hands in front of you with one hand on top of the other and both of your palms facing down. Slide your top hand back to the wrist of the bottom hand. Now move your bottom hand to the top, and repeat the sliding motion. It should look like you are putting on gloves.

 **hat:** Pat the top of your head twice. It should look like you are showing where a hat is worn.

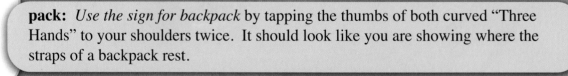 **pack:** *Use the sign for backpack* by tapping the thumbs of both curved "Three Hands" to your shoulders twice. It should look like you are showing where the straps of a backpack rest.

pants: Touch the palms of your hands to the front of your legs, then pull your hands up to your waist as you touch your fingertips to your thumbs. Now repeat this movement. It should look like you are pulling up a pair of pants.

robe: There are several different ways to sign "robe." Some people use the sign for "coat." Others sign "dress" using the "R Hands." Another option is to simply fingerspell R-O-B-E.

shirt: Use your pointer finger and thumb to tug at a small piece of your shirt near your shoulder. It should look like you are showing someone the item of clothing you are talking about.

shoes: Hold both "S Hands" in front of your body and tap them against each other twice. It should look like you are clicking the heels of your shoes together.

shorts: Bend your hands at the large knuckle and touch the pinky finger side of your hands to your thighs with your palms facing up. Now, slide your hands back and forth across your legs. It should look like you are showing the length of a pair of shorts.

socks: Hold your pointer fingers in front of you with the sides touching and the tips pointing down. Now rub your fingers together a couple of times in opposite directions, so one finger moves down toward your feet, while the other moves up. It should look like you are rubbing your cold feet together.

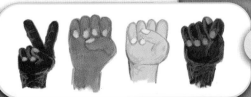

vest: Fingerspell V-E-S-T.

Fun Facts about ASL

If you know you are going to repeat a fingerspelled word during a conversation or story, you can fingerspell it the first time, then quickly show a related ASL sign to use when the word comes up again. For example, you can fingerspell V-E-S-T, then sign "shirt." This shows your signing partner that you mean "vest" the next time you sign "shirt."

Most sign language dictionaries describe how a sign looks for a right-handed signer. If you are left-handed, you would modify the instructions so the signs feel more comfortable to you. For example, to sign the second part of "boot," a left-handed signer would rest the right arm in front of the body and tap the left hand on the middle of the right arm.

Signing is fun to learn and can be helpful in many ways. Kids who sign often become better readers and stronger spellers than kids who don't sign. Even babies can learn to use sign language to communicate before they can talk. And when you learn to sign, you can communicate with many people who are deaf.

6 7 8 9 10

Signing Activities

Sign Language Concentration: On the front of 13 blank index cards, write one word from the ASL glossary. On the front of 13 more cards, draw a picture to go along with that word. Leave the back of all the cards blank. Shuffle the 26 cards and lay them all facedown in a pattern of columns and rows in front of you. The first player turns over two cards. If the cards match, that player must make the sign for the word shown on the cards. If the player makes the correct sign, he or she gets to keep the matching cards. If the cards don't match, or the player cannot make the correct sign, both cards should be turned back over, and it is the next player's turn. Play continues until all the cards are matched. The player with the most cards wins.

Sign Language Memory Game: This is a fun game for a classroom or a group of friends to play together. Stand in a circle and choose someone to begin. The first player makes the sign for one item of clothing, like a hat. The second player repeats the sign made by the first player and adds a new sign, so the second player signs hat and coat. The third player repeats the first two signs and adds a new sign, so the third player signs hat, coat, and shirt. A player is out and must sit down if they cannot repeat the string of signs required on their turn. Play continues with the next player wherever the game left off. The last player left standing wins!

Additional Resources

Further Reading

Costello, Elaine, PhD. *Random House Webster's Concise American Sign Language Dictionary.* Bantam, 2002.

Heller, Lora. *Sign Language for Kids.* Sterling, 2004.

Sign2Me. *Pick Me Up! Fun Songs for Learning Signs (A CD and Activity Guide).* Northlight Communications, 2003.

Warner, Penny. *Signing Fun.* Gallaudet University Press, 2006.

Web Sites

To learn more about ASL, visit ABDO Group online at **www.abdopublishing.com**. Web sites about ASL are featured on our Book Links page. These links are routinely monitored and updated to provide the most current information available.